PAIR-IT BOOKS

We Are All Glad!

Written by Margaret Fetty
Illustrated by Karen Bell

STECK-VAUGHN
ELEMENTARY · SECONDARY · ADULT · LIBRARY

A Harcourt Company

www.steck-vaughn.com

He feels sad.

Now he feels glad!

She feels sad.

Now she feels glad!

He feels sad.

Now he feels glad!

Now we all feel glad!